This book belongs to:

_____

_____

_____

_____

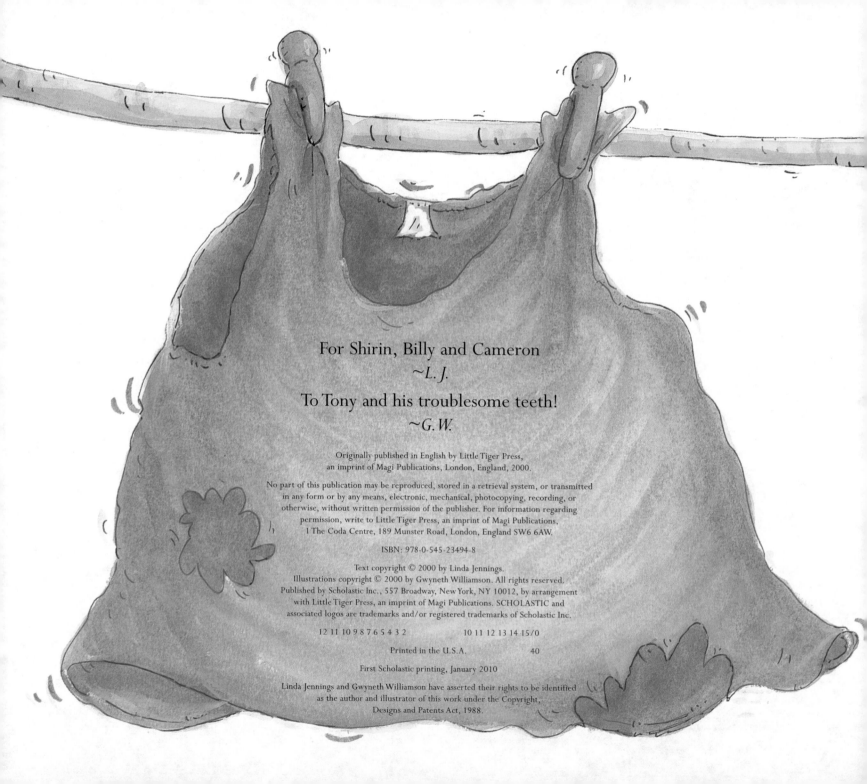

For Shirin, Billy and Cameron
~L. J.

To Tony and his troublesome teeth!
~G. W.

Originally published in English by Little Tiger Press,
an imprint of Magi Publications, London, England, 2000.

ISBN: 978-0-545-23494-8

12 11 10 9 8 7 6 5 4 3 2   10 11 12 13 14 15/0

Printed in the U.S.A.   40

First Scholastic printing, January 2010

Linda Jennings and Gwyneth Williamson have asserted their rights to be identified
as the author and illustrator of this work under the Copyright,
Designs and Patents Act, 1988.

Tooth
on the Loose!

Linda Jennings and Gwyneth Williamson

Originally published as
Titus's Troublesome Tooth

SCHOLASTIC INC.
New York Toronto London Auckland
Sydney Mexico City New Delhi Hong Kong

Titus the Goat ate everything.
He ate carrots and cabbages.

He ate dandelions
and dockleaves.

He ate prickly,
tickly thistles . . .

and he even ate Farmer
Harry's pants and vests
off the washing line!

Titus absolutely
loved eating –
until one day . . .

he woke up with
a terrible pain.

He didn't want
his breakfast . . .

and he didn't want to munch
and crunch the apples
in the orchard.

He wasn't even tempted to
nibble at Mrs Harry's nightdress.
Titus felt as miserable as . . .

well, as miserable as a goat with a toothache!
He was a very grouchy, grumbly goat indeed.

"That's a troublesome tooth," said Derry
the Donkey. "Open your mouth and I'll
pull it out with my big, strong teeth."

Titus shook from his
horns to the tip of his tail.
"Ooh-er, no thanks," he bleated.
He ran and ran and grouched
and grumbled . . .

until he reached the farmyard.

"That's a troublesome tooth," said Sadie
the Hen. "Open your mouth and I'll peck
it out with my nice, sharp beak."
Titus quivered on all four hooves.
"Ooh-er, no thanks," he cried.
Titus ran and ran and grouched
and grumbled . . .

until he reached the barn. "That's a troublesome tooth," said Polly the Cat. "Open your mouth and I'll scratch it out with my long, shiny claws."

Titus trembled from
his white beard to his
furry bottom.
"Ooh-er, no thanks,"
he shouted.

Titus ran and ran and
grouched and grumbled . . .

until he reached
the meadow.
"That's a troublesome
tooth," said Basil the Bull. "Open your mouth and I'll
butt it out with my hard, curly horns."

All Titus's teeth chattered and
rattled – even the bad one!
"Ooh-er, no thanks," he sobbed.
Titus ran and ran and grouched
and grumbled . . .

until he reached the duck pond.

"That's a troublesome tooth," said Daphne the
Duck. "Open your mouth and I'll tug it out with
some duckweed."

Titus shook so much that he nearly fell into the water.

"Ooh-er, no thanks," he yelled.

Titus ran and ran and grouched and grumbled . . .

until he found himself right back in the farmyard again. "Don't worry," said Sadie the Hen.

"Farmer Harry will get rid of that troublesome tooth for you, because he's called the Vet!

"The Vet!"
shouted Titus.

THE VET!

He quivered and he shivered,
he trembled and he shook.
His teeth rattled and
chattered – even the bad one.
"No way do I want *the Vet!*"

Titus ran and ran

and grouched

and grumbled until . . .

and the troublesome
tooth fell out at last!